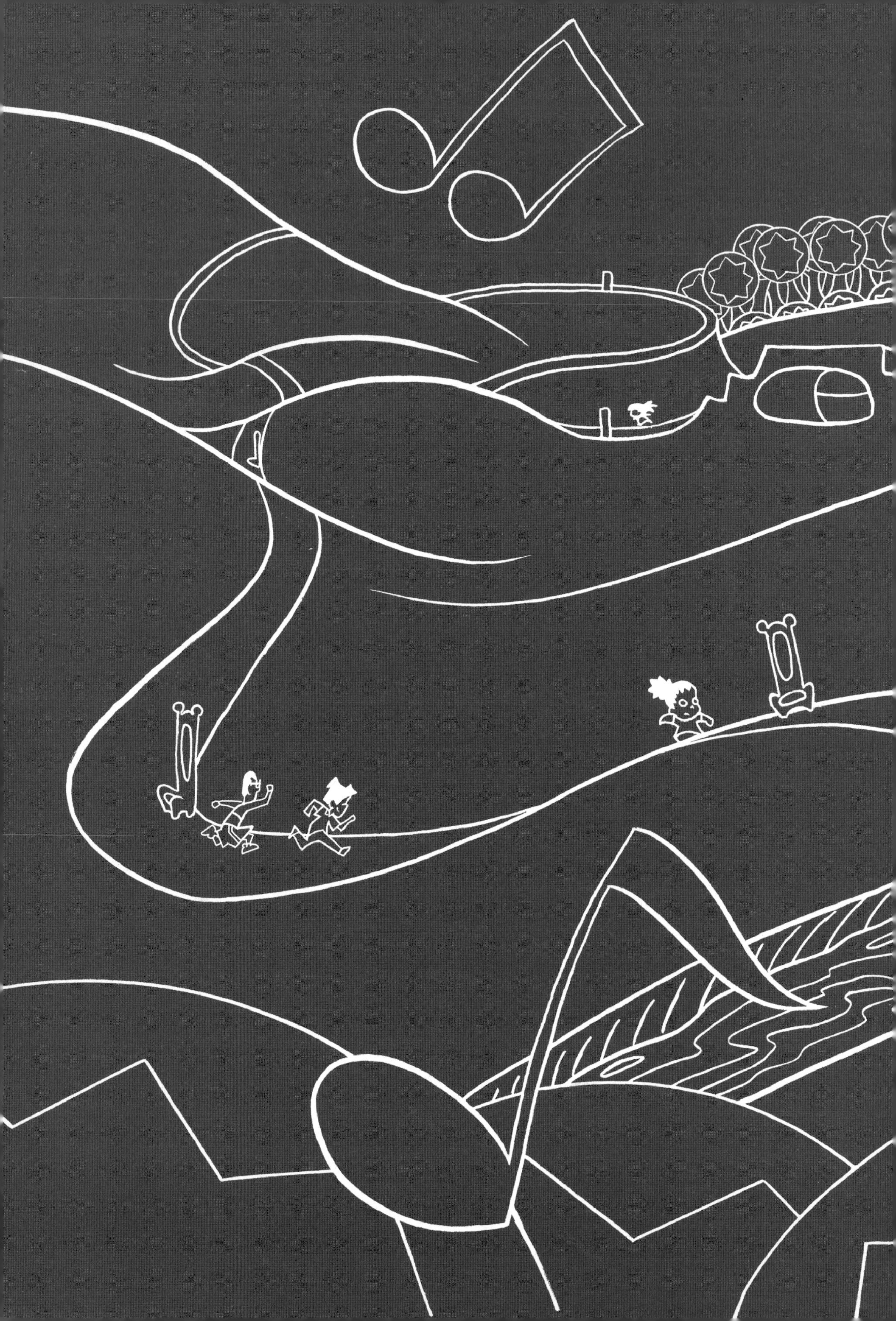

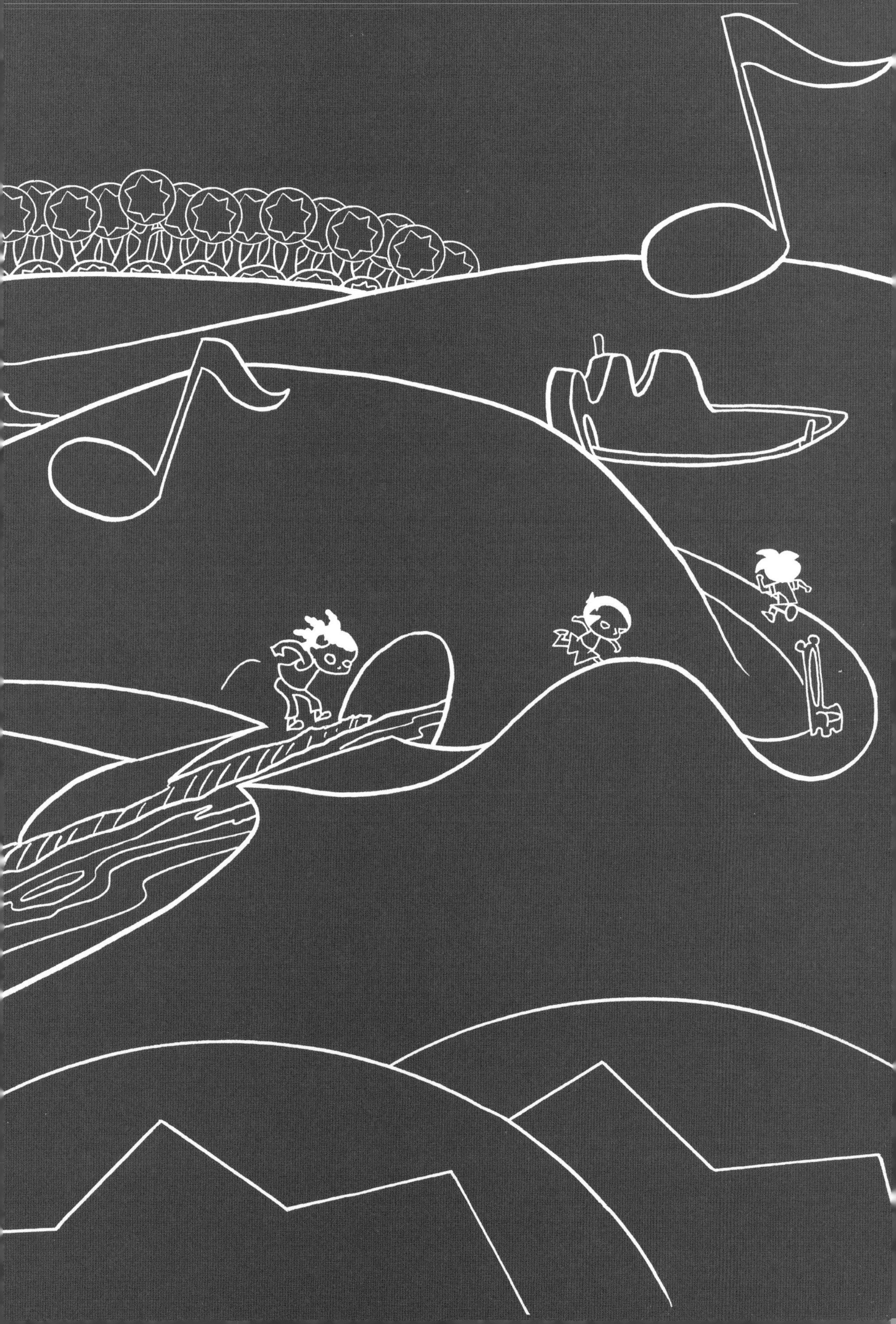

Game for ADVENTURE
Belinda the Unbeatable

A GRAPHIC NOVEL
Lee Nordling & Scott Roberts

Graphic Universe™ • Minneapolis

For Cheri,
still and forever (which is a really long time)
the love of all of my lives.
And a special thanks to Greg Hunter & Danielle Carnito
for helping to shepherd our vision for this story.
– Lee Nordling

To Bella,
the collie who wondered how Copper the corgi got his name into that last book.
You're still the fluffiest, Bella.
– Scott Roberts

Lee Nordling is a two-time Eisner Award nominee
and award-winning writer, editor, creative director,
and book packager. He worked on staff at
Disney Publishing, DC Comics, and
Nickelodeon Magazine.

Scott Roberts is a two-time Eisner and Ignatz Award nominee,
graphic novel artist and writer, illustrator, character designer, script doctor,
and colorist. He's the creator of the comic book *Patty Cake* and a writer/artist for
Spongebob Comics. He also draws the syndicated comics *Working Daze* and
Maria's Day and colors the classic Sunday comic *Prince Valiant*.
Scott worked on the *Rugrats* comic strip with Lee Nordling.

Story and script by Lee Nordling
Art by Scott Roberts
Color by Scott Roberts and Flavio B. Silva/Magic Eye Studios

Belinda the Unbeatable © 2017 by Lee Nordling & Scott Roberts

Belinda the Unbeatable and the Game for Adventure series
were placed, designed, and produced by The Pack.

Graphic Universe™ is a trademark of Lerner Publishing
Group, Inc.

Graphic Universe™
A division of Lerner Publishing Group, Inc.
241 First Avenue North
Minneapolis, MN 55401 USA

For reading levels and more information, look up this title at
www.lernerbooks.com.

Library of Congress Cataloging-in-Publication Data

Names: Nordling, Lee, author. | Roberts, Scott, 1956–
illustrator.
Title: Belinda the unbeatable / Lee Nordling, Scott Roberts.
Description: Minneapolis : Graphic Universe, [2017] |
Series: Game for adventure | Summary: "Two best
friends take part in a game of musical chairs. There's
Belinda, a natural competitor with a good heart, and her
shy friend Barbara. When the game starts, their school
gym morphs into a colorful obstacle course" –Provided
by publisher.
Identifiers: LCCN 2016035925 (print) | LCCN 2017008401
(ebook) | ISBN 9781512413311 (lb : alk. paper) | ISBN
9781512448801 (eb pdf) | ISBN 9781512454130 (pbk.)
Subjects: LCSH: Graphic novels. | CYAC: Graphic novels.
| Best friends–Fiction. | Friendship–Fiction. | Games–
Fiction. | Schools–Fiction.
Classification: LCC PZ7.7.N67 Be 2017 (print) | LCC
PZ7.7.N67 (ebook) | DDC 741.5/973–dc23

LC record available at https://lccn.loc.gov/2016035925

Manufactured in the United States of America
1-39789-21326-4/4/2017

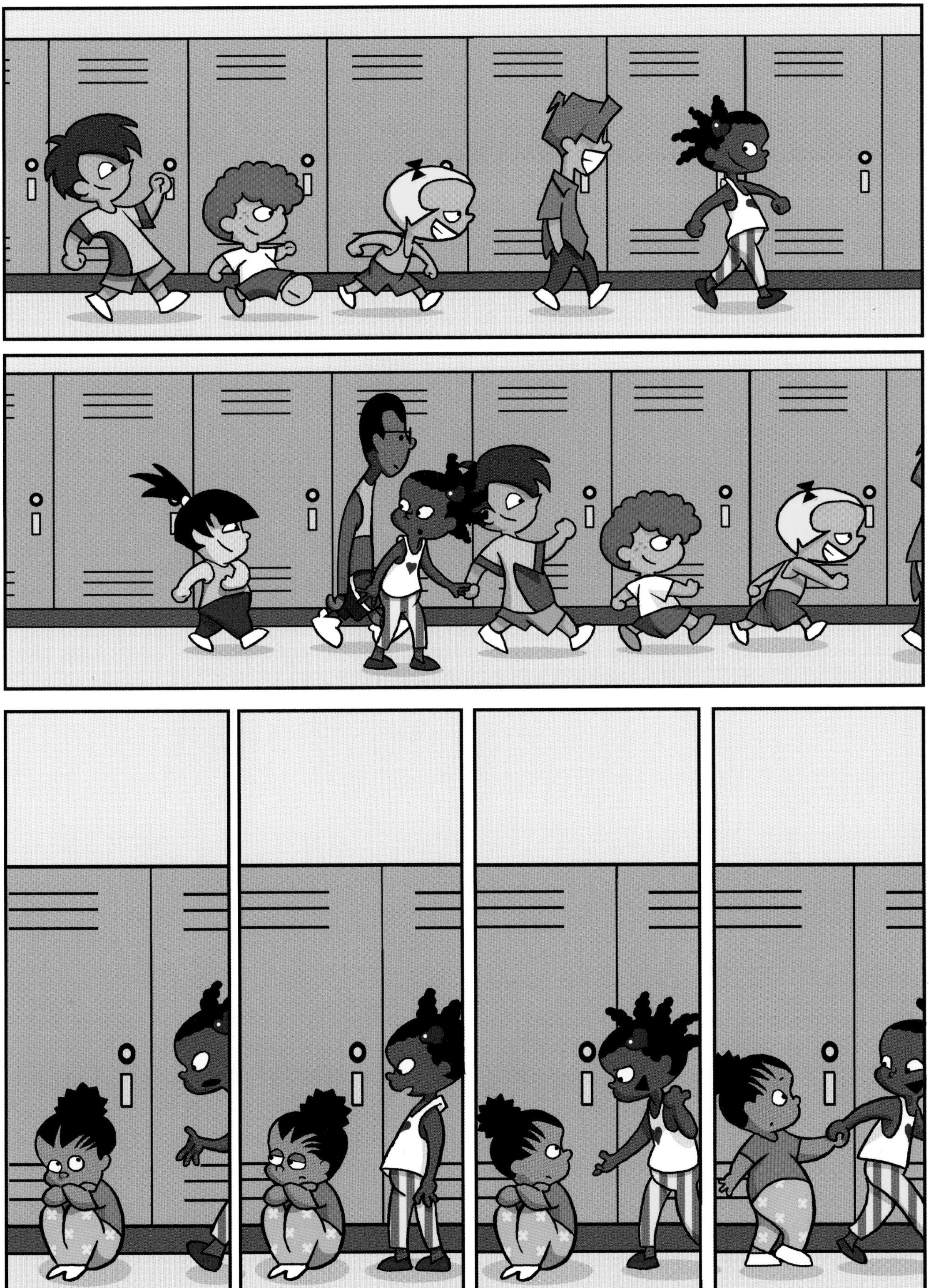

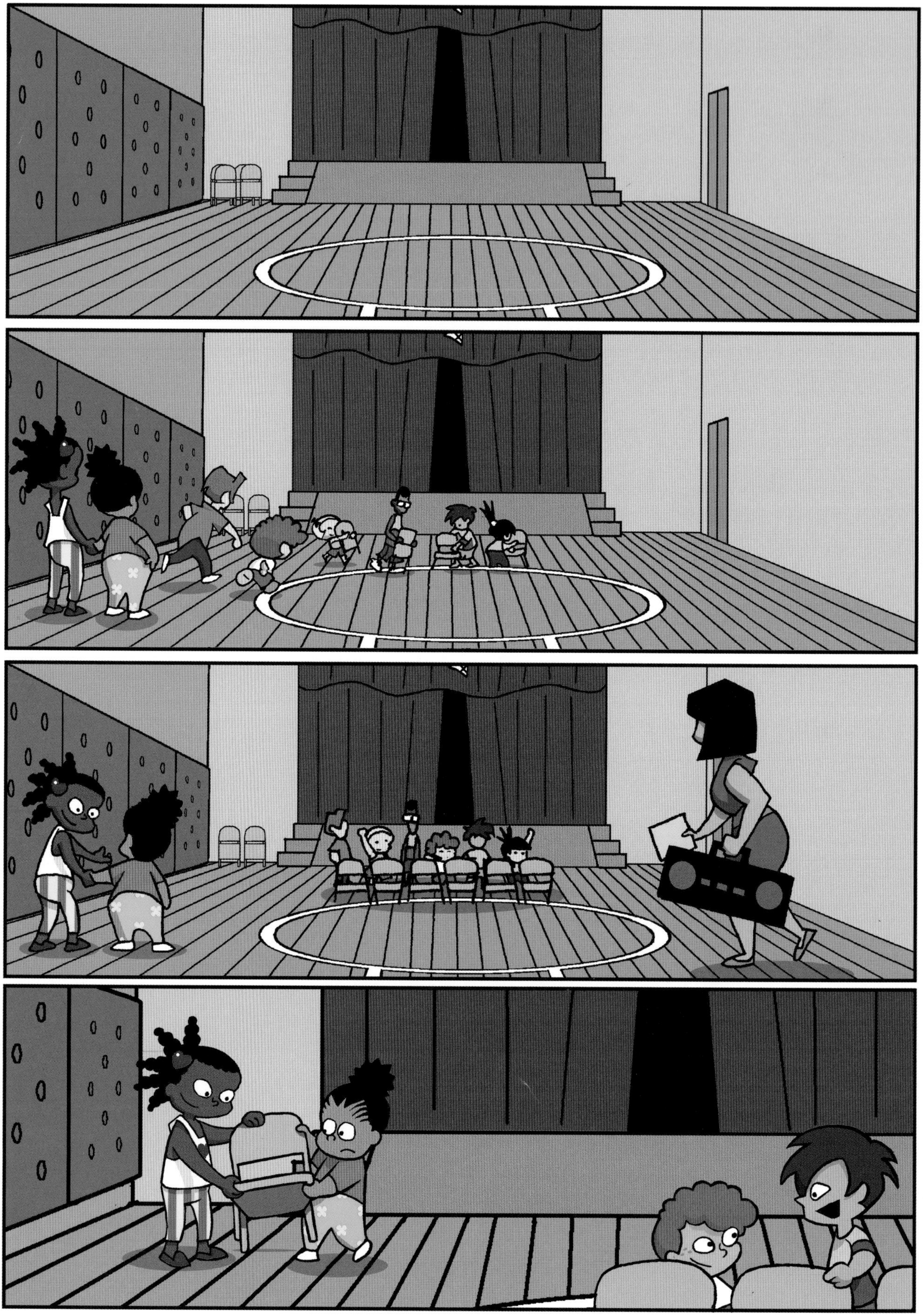

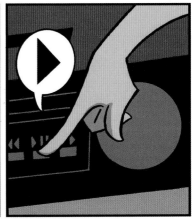

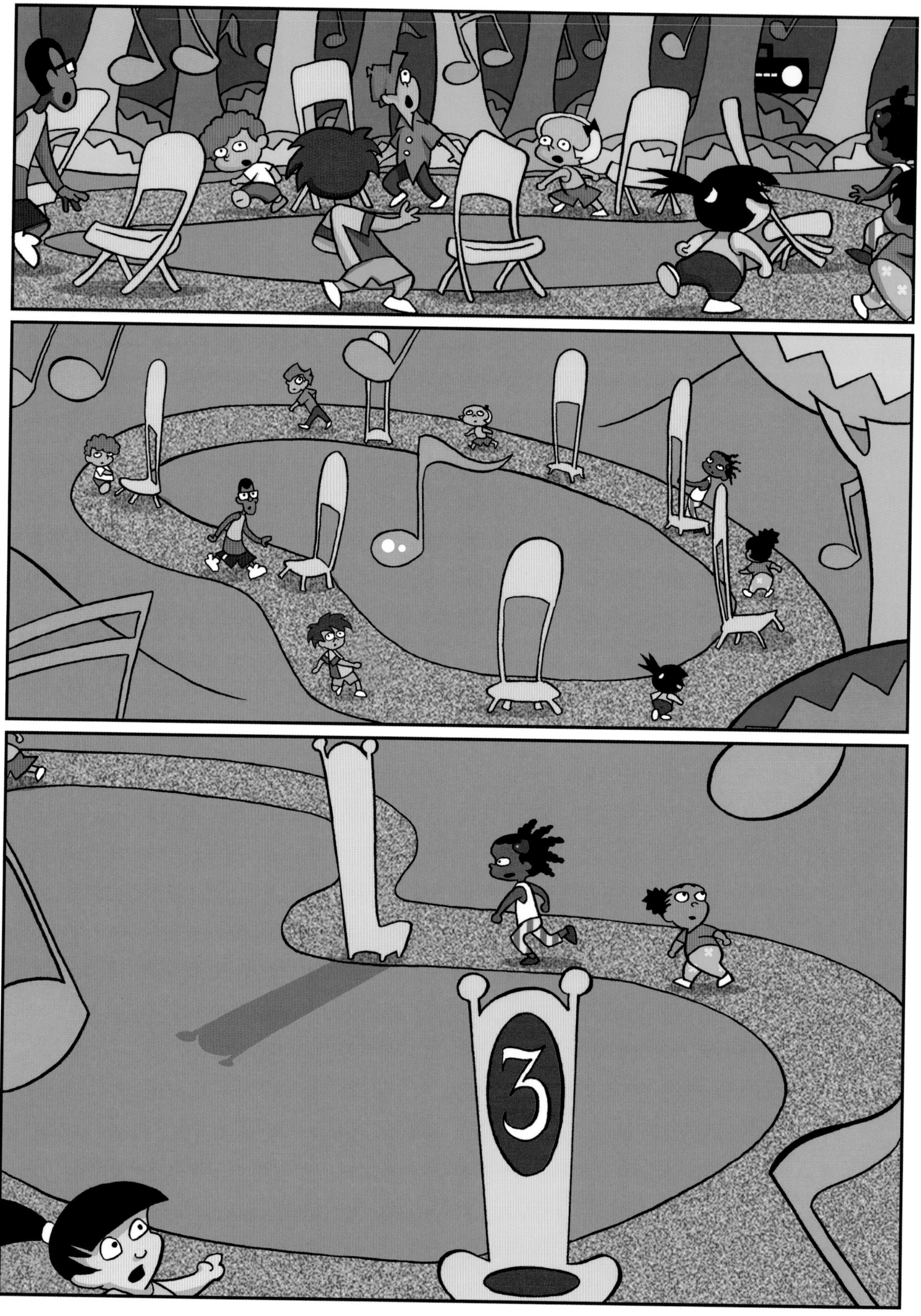
3

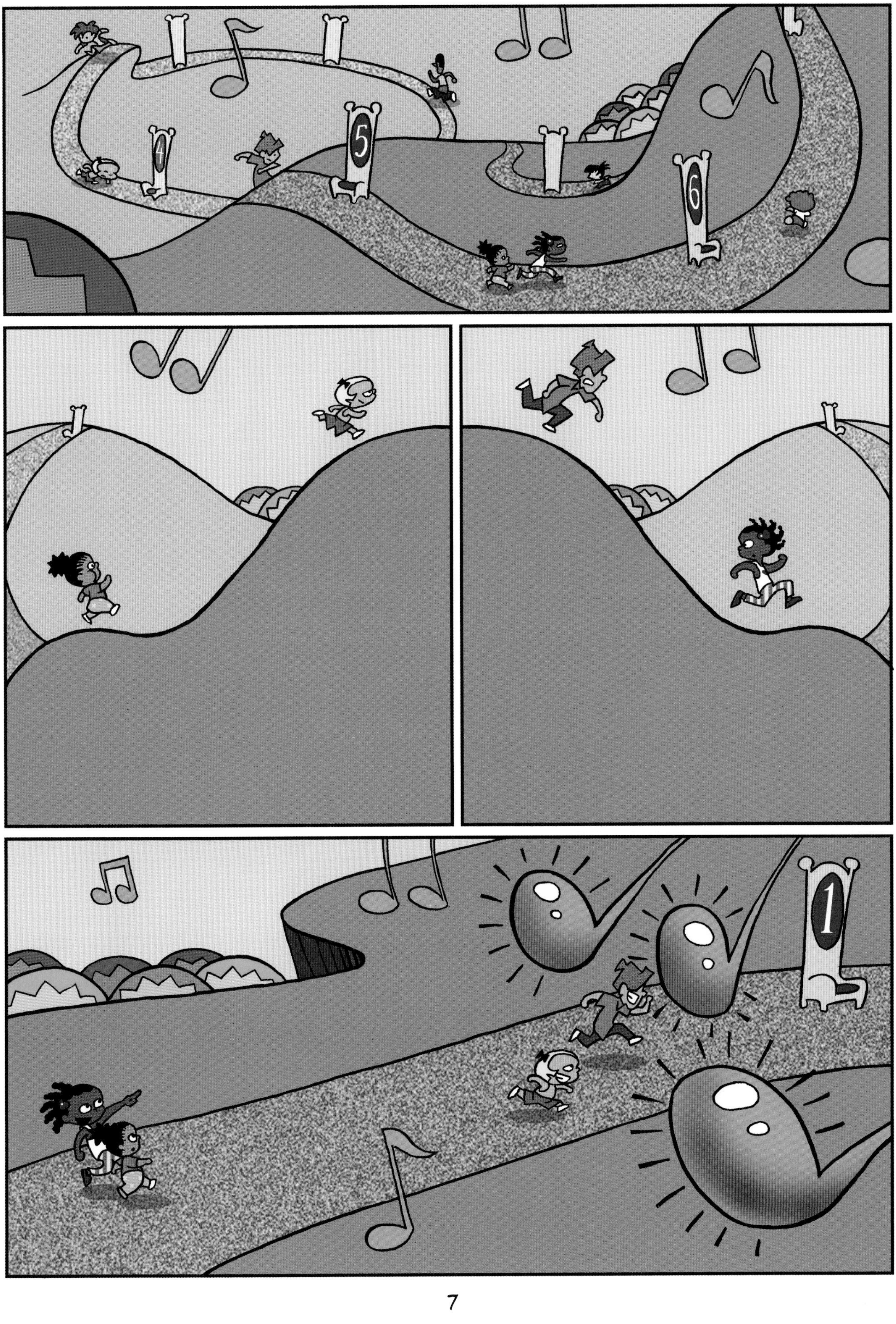
4
5
6
1

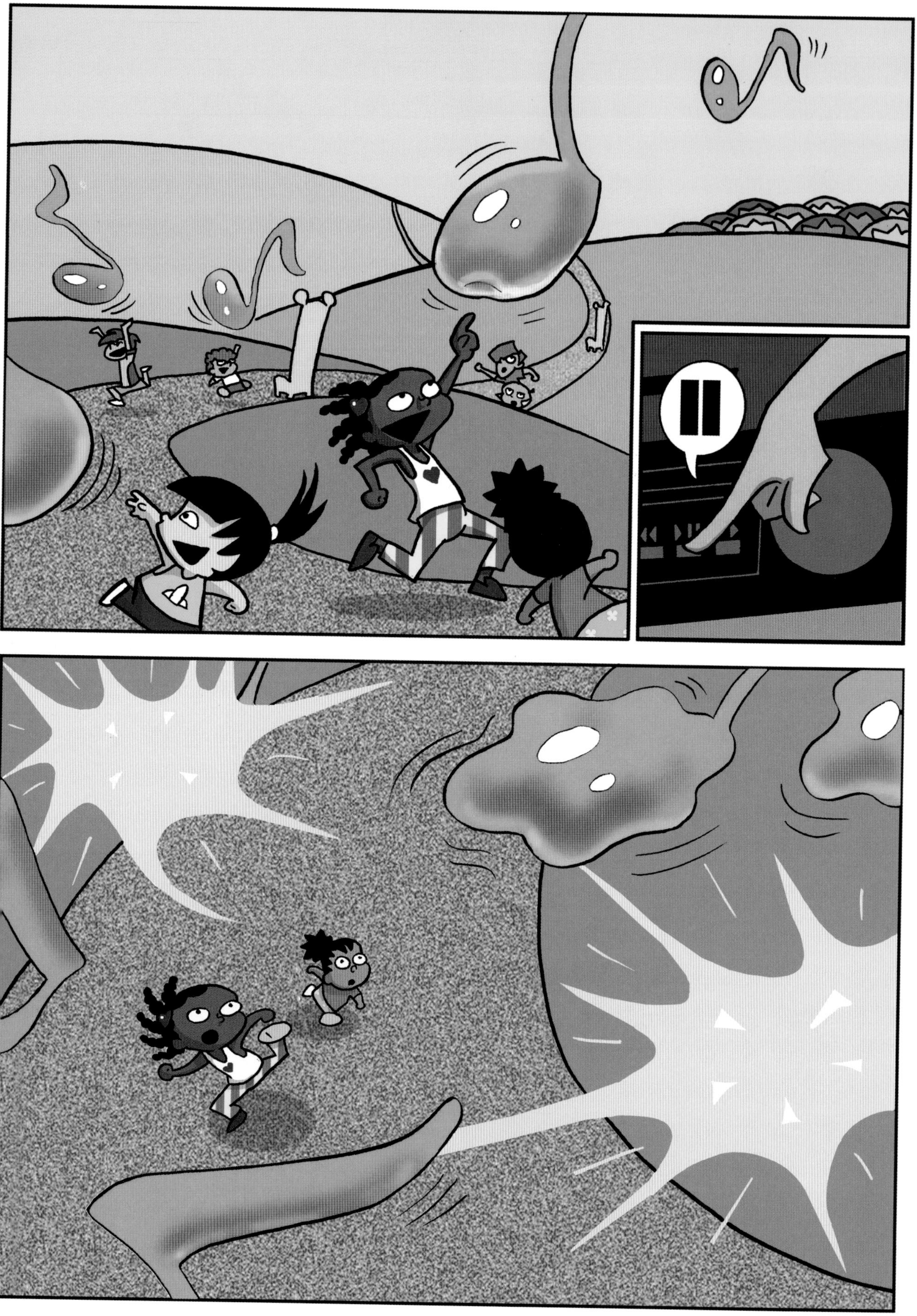

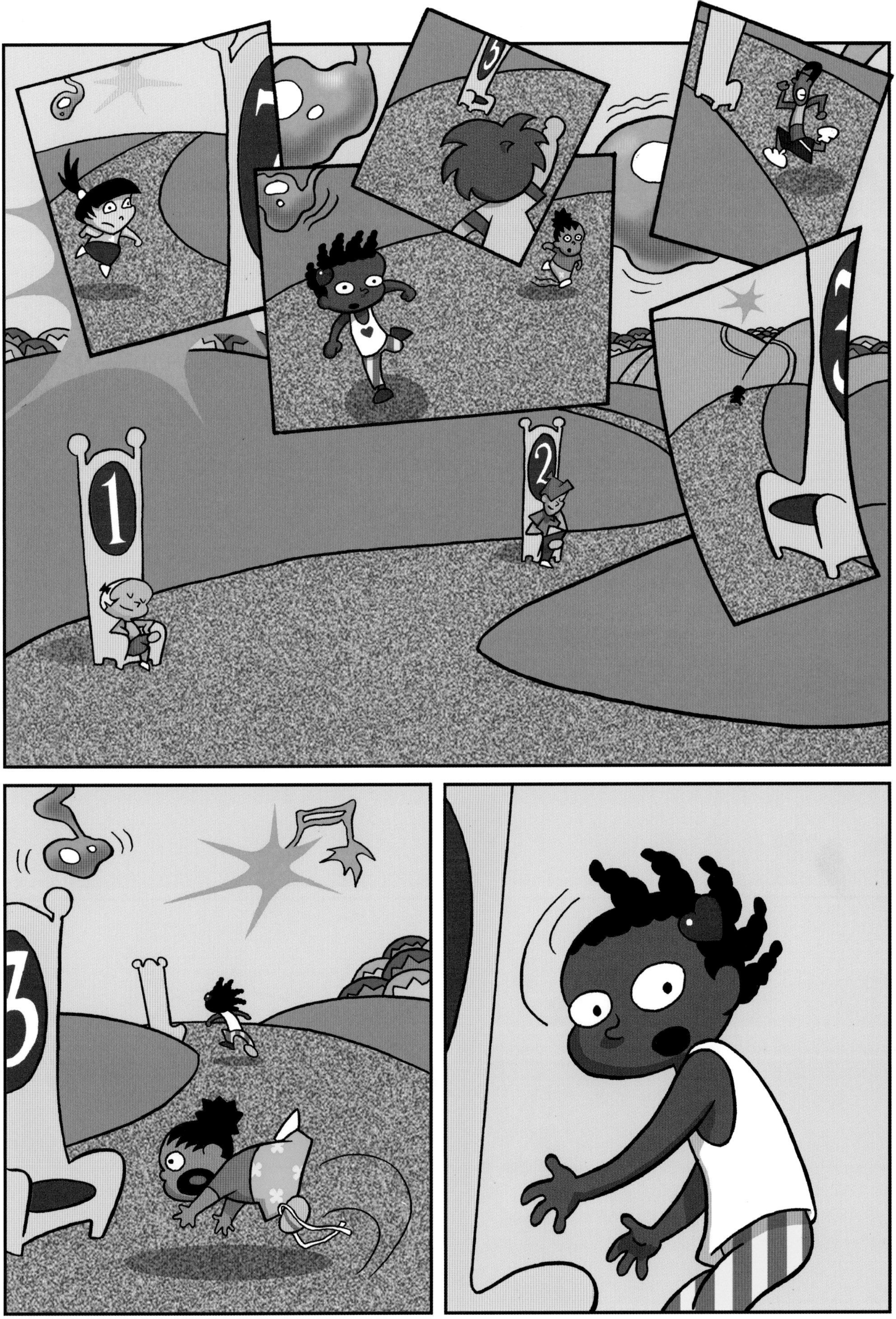
1
2
3

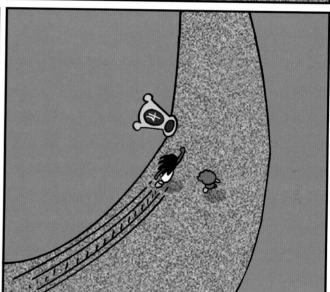

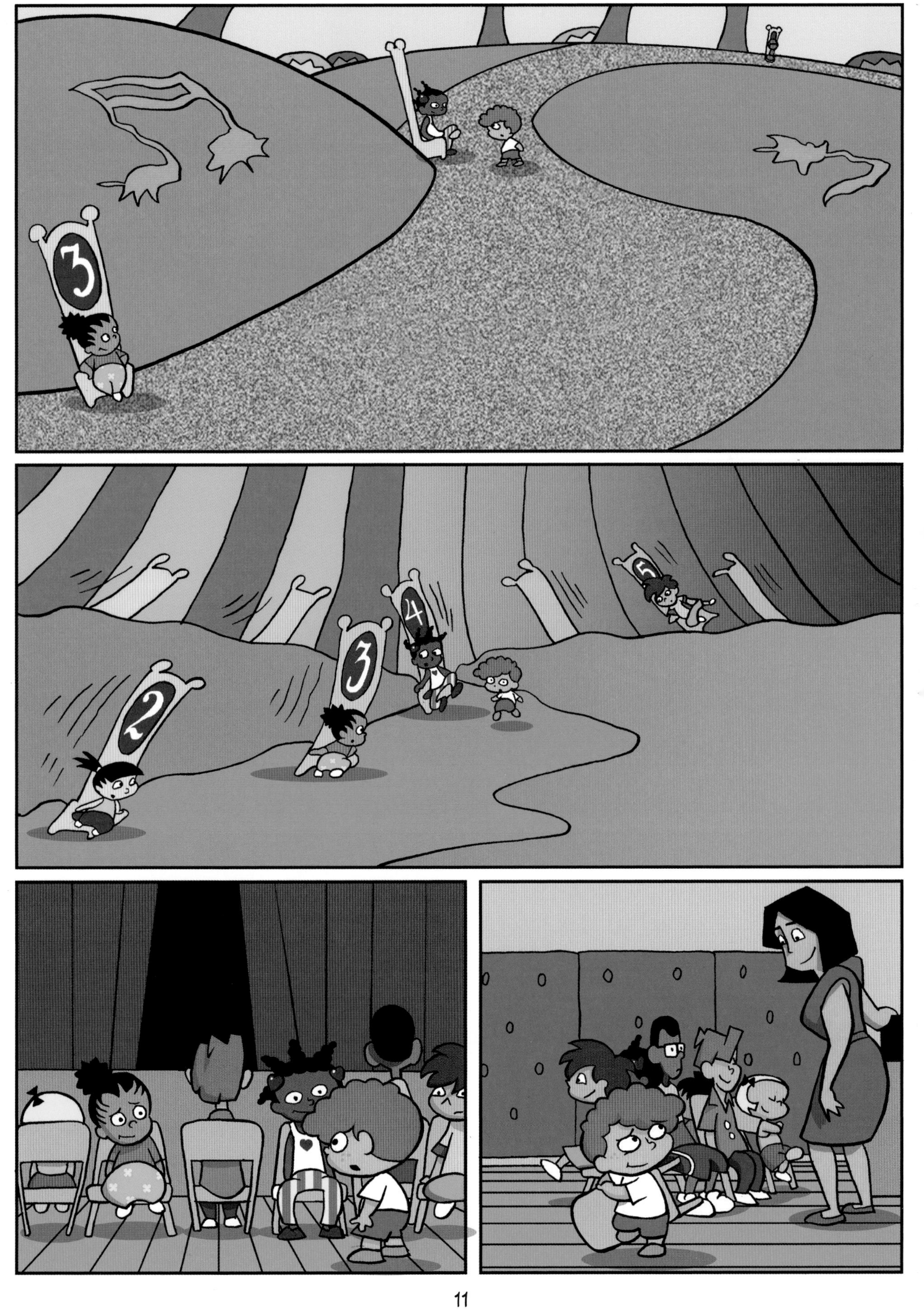
3
2
3
4
5

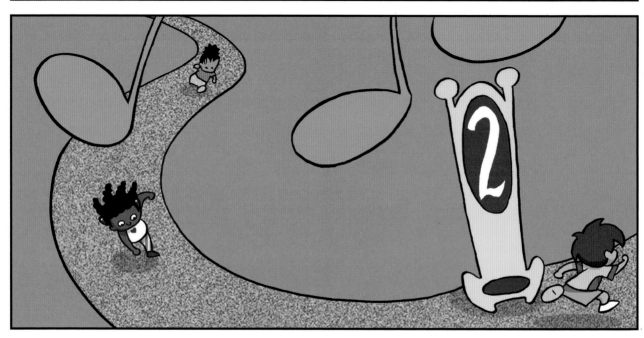

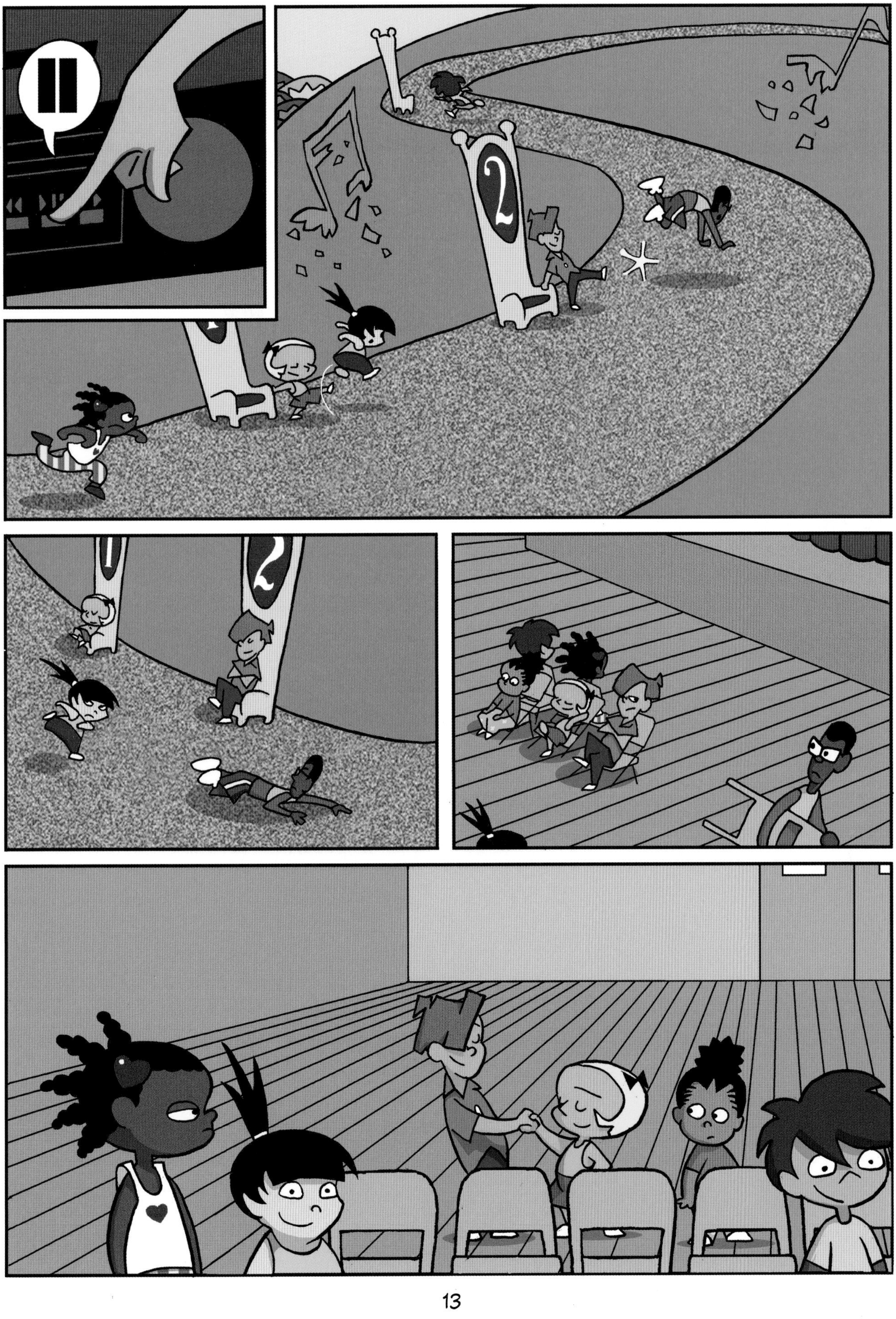

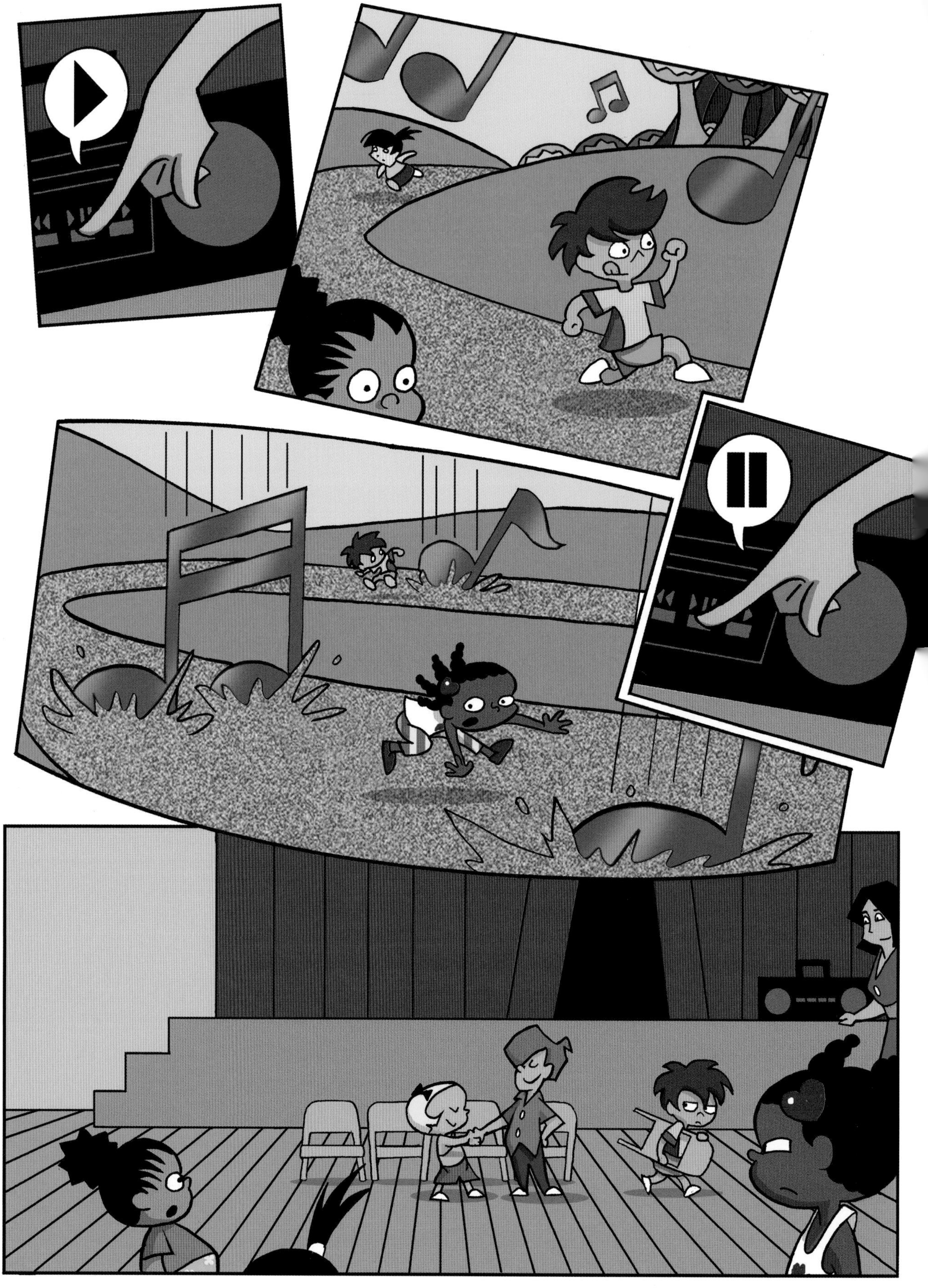

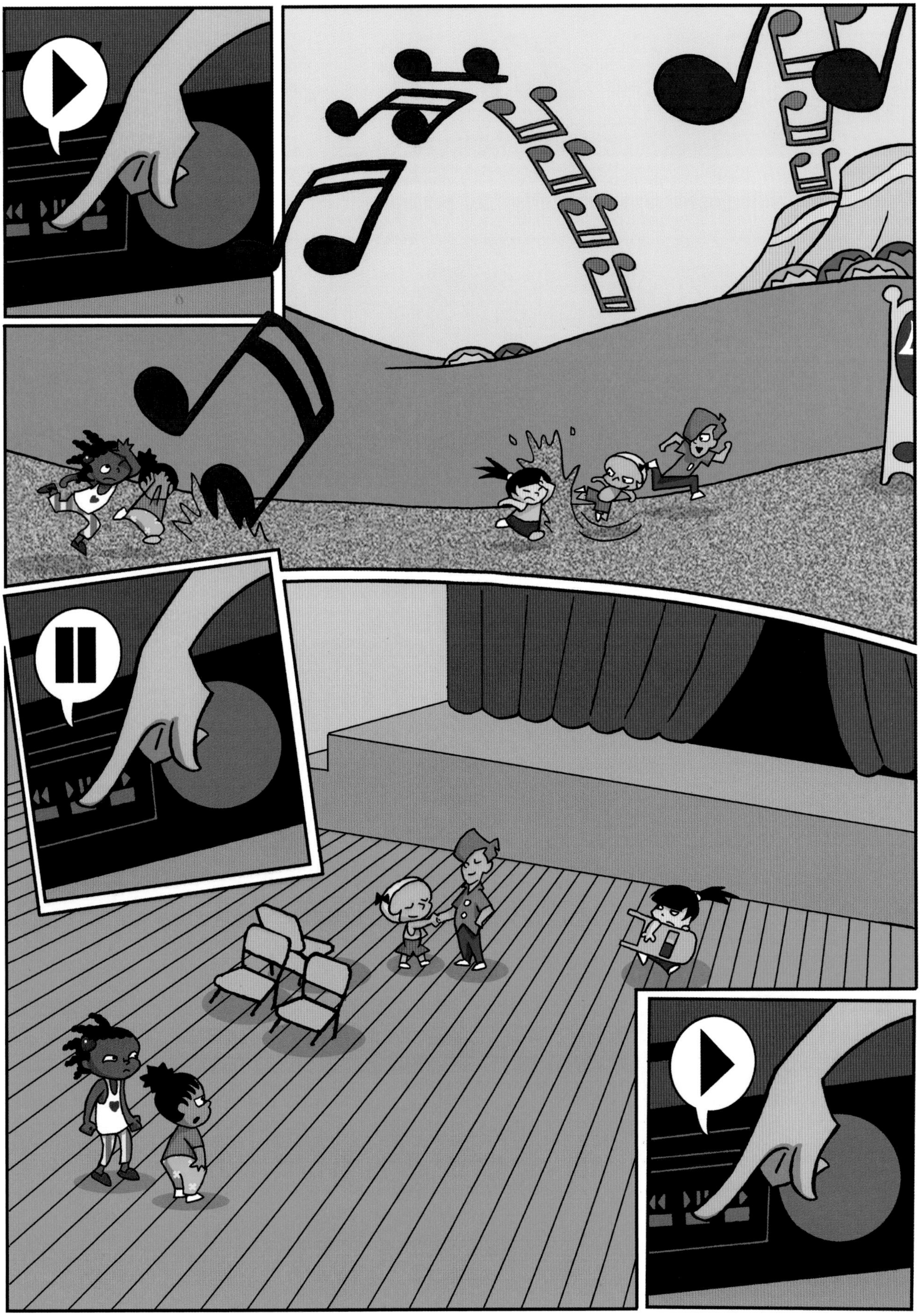

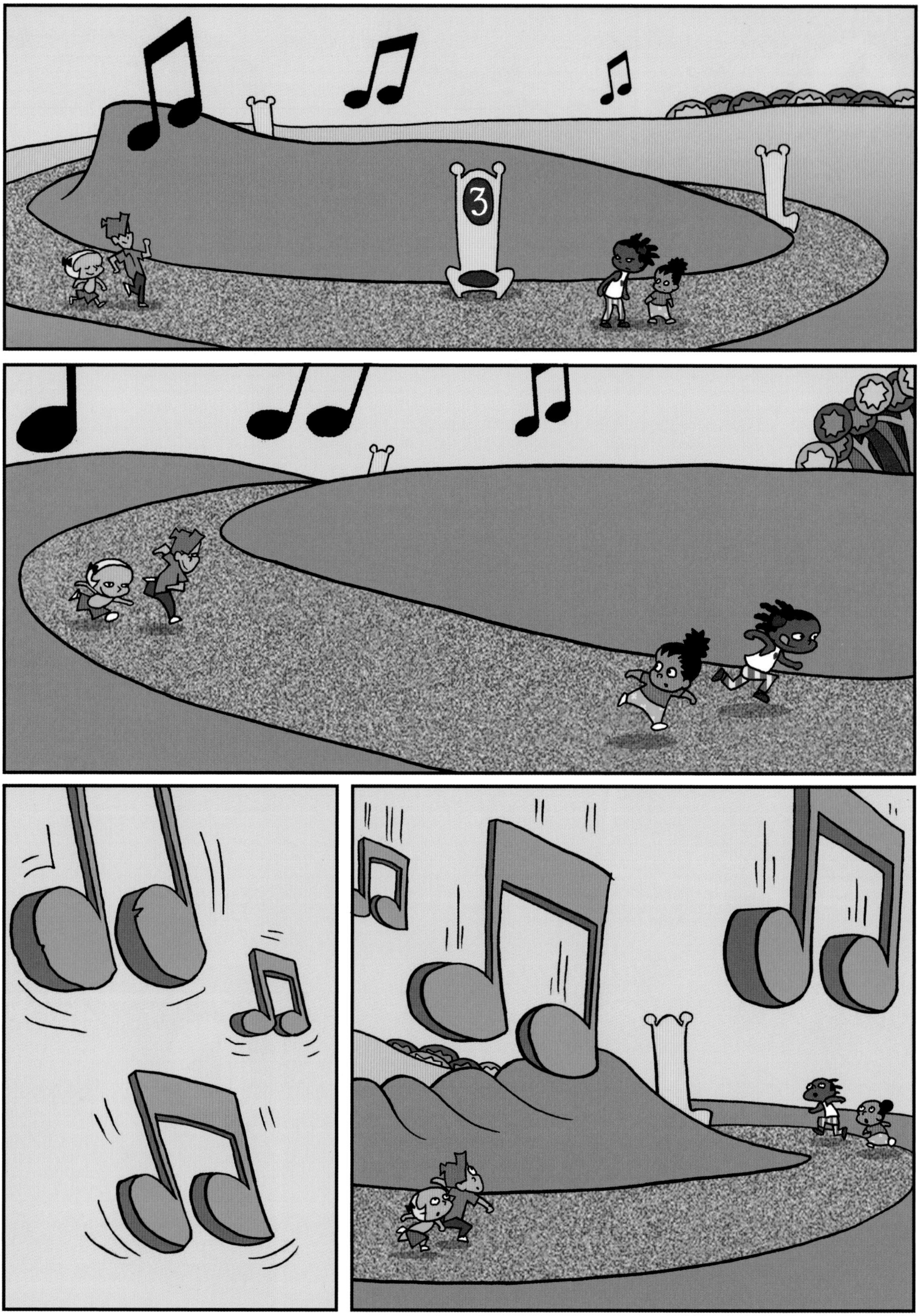
3

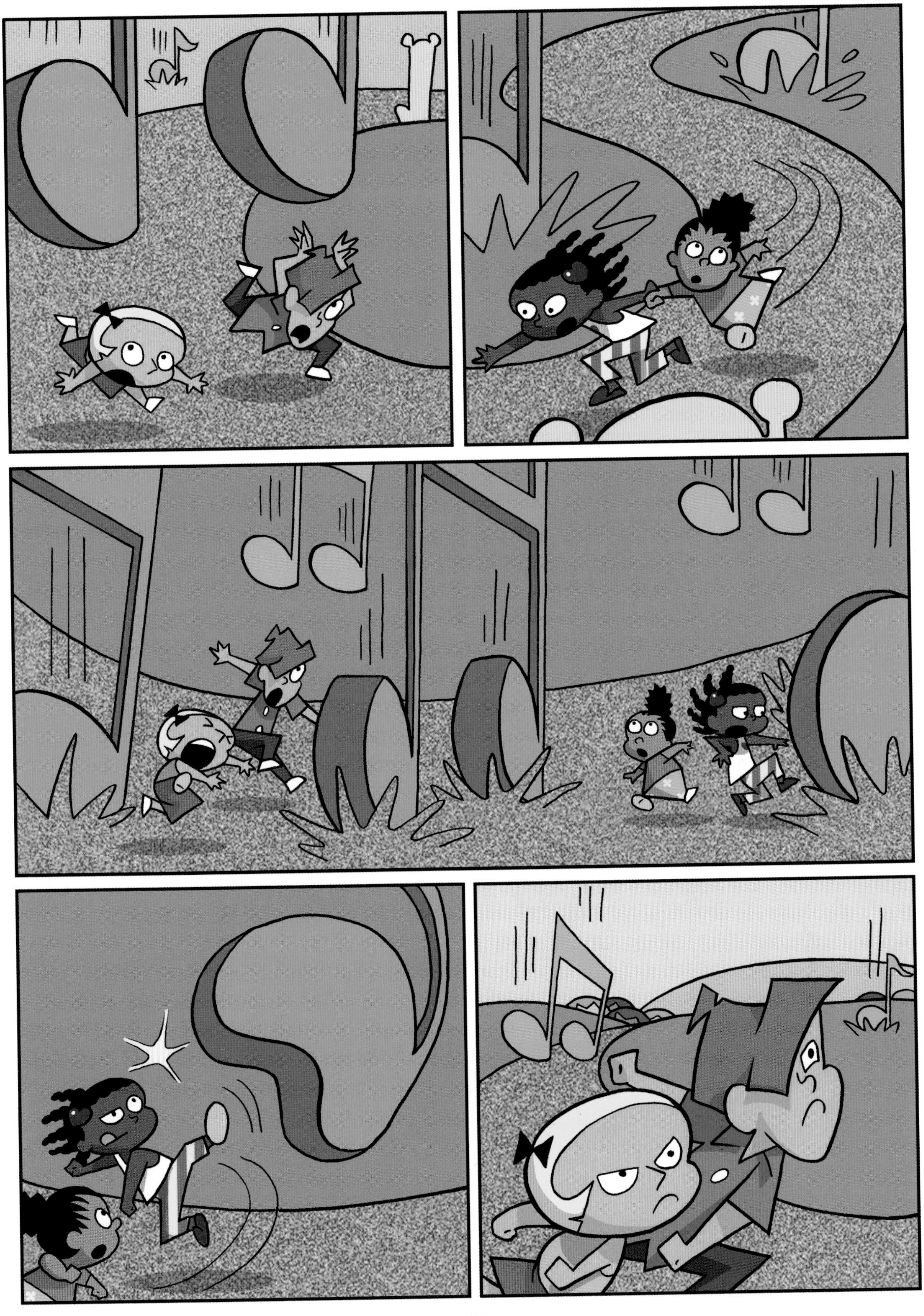

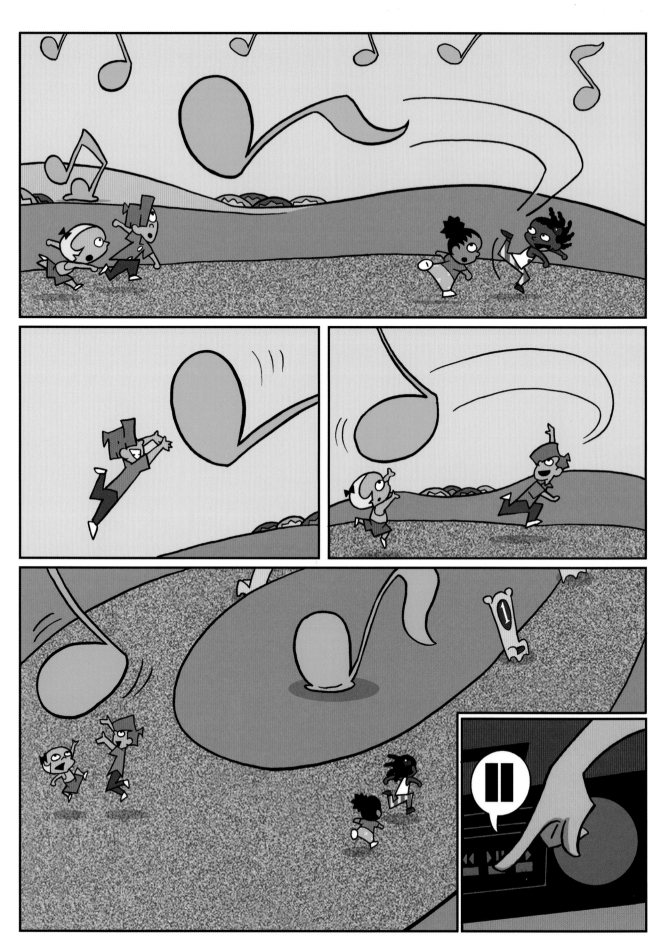

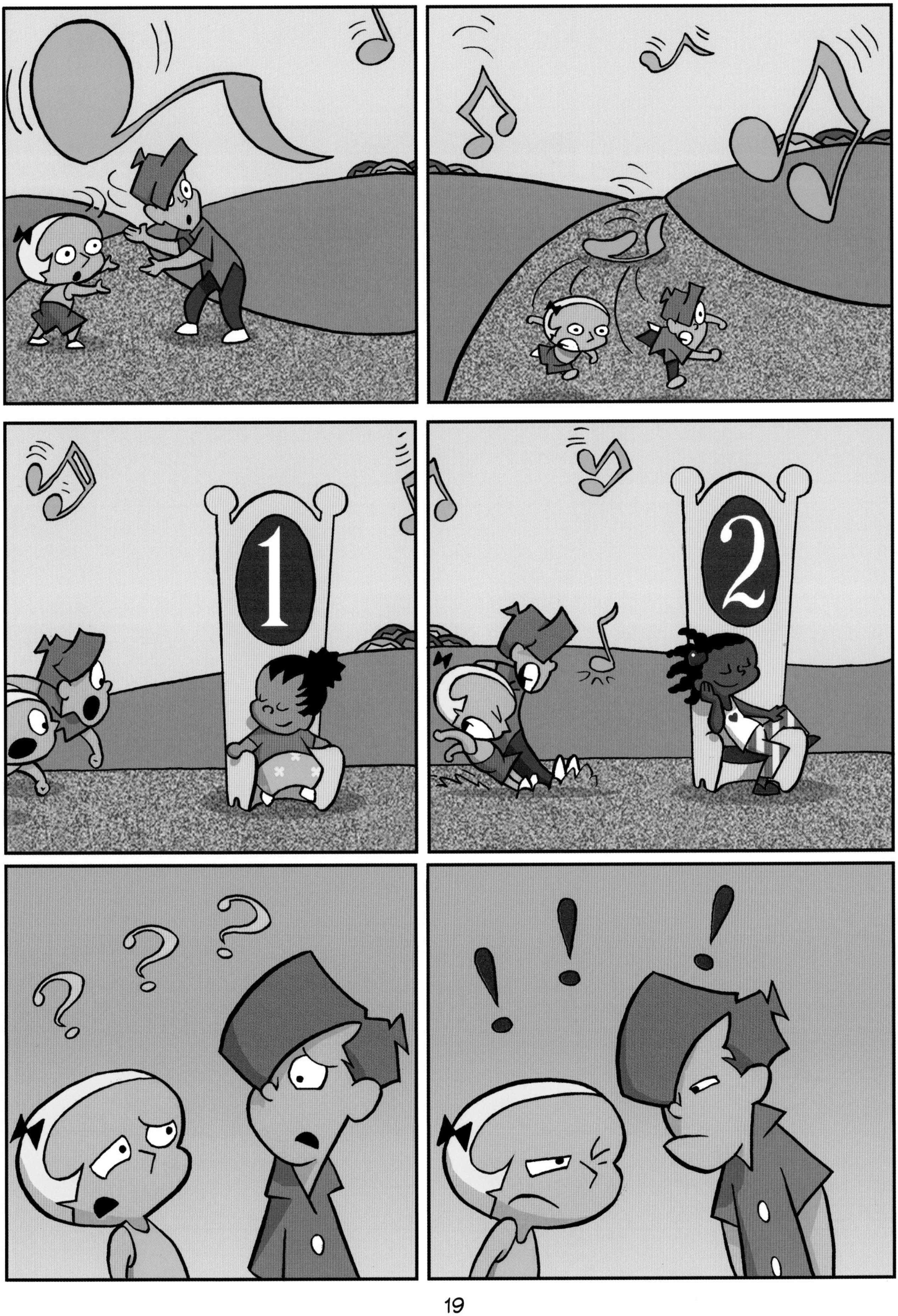
1
2

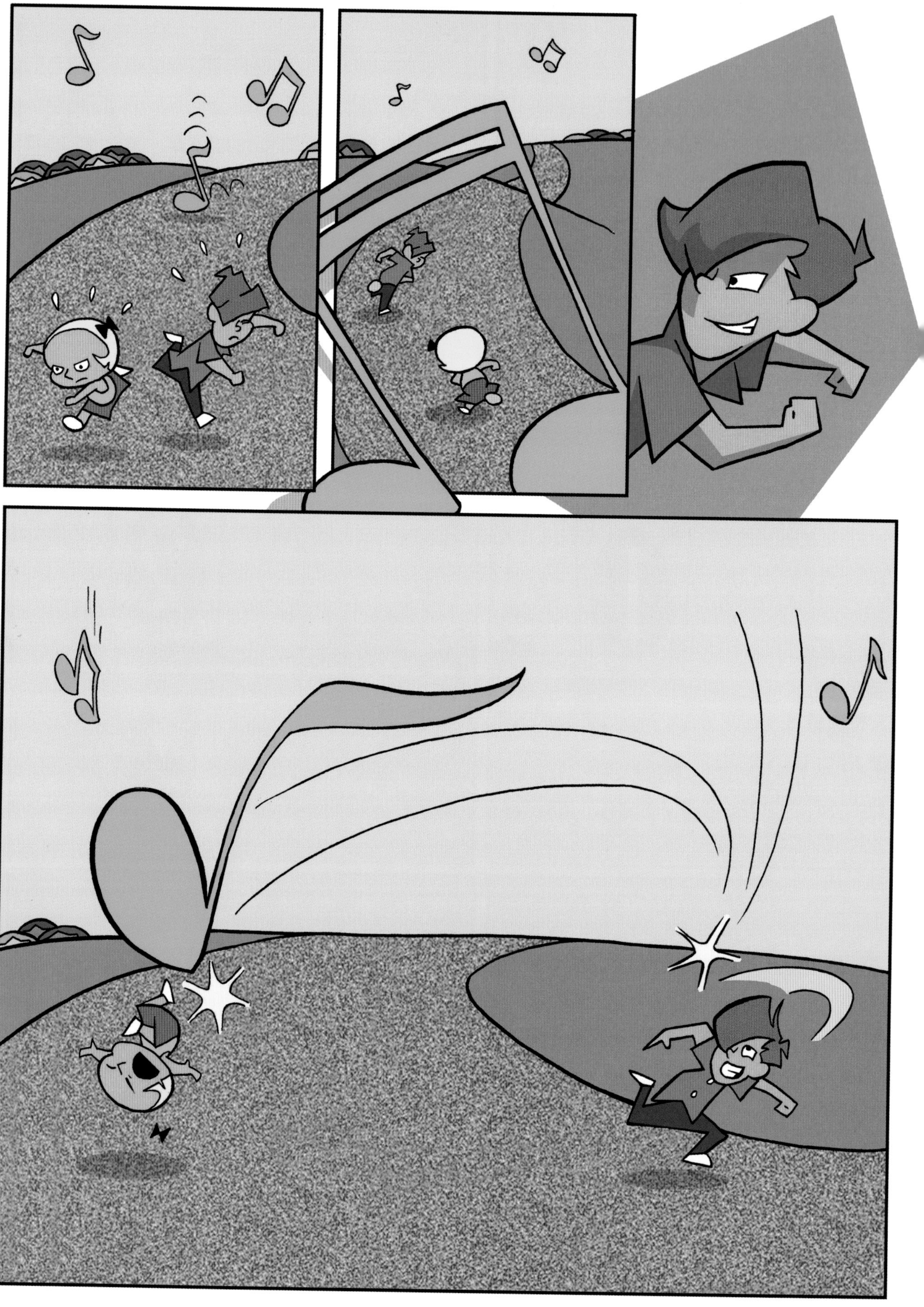

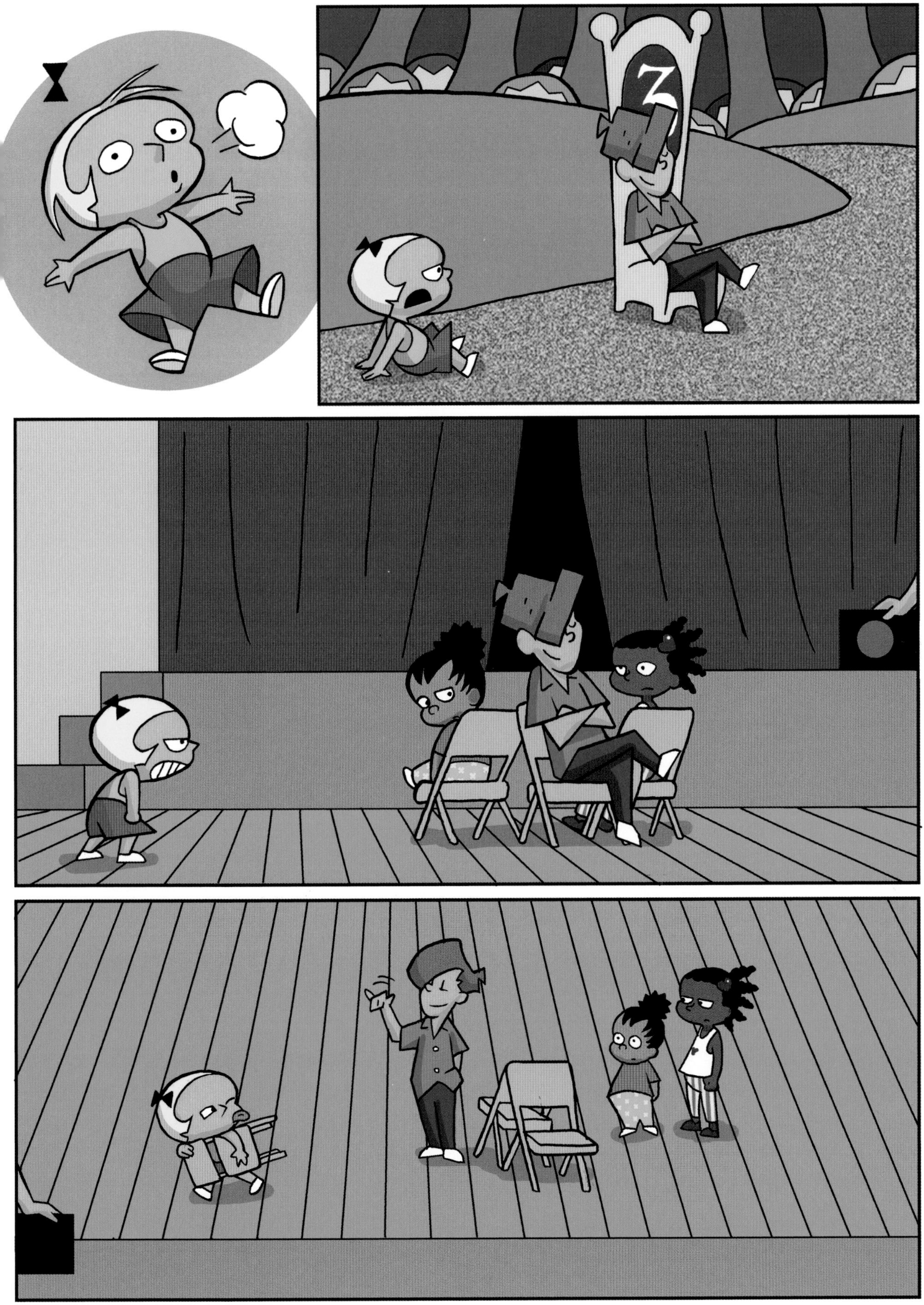

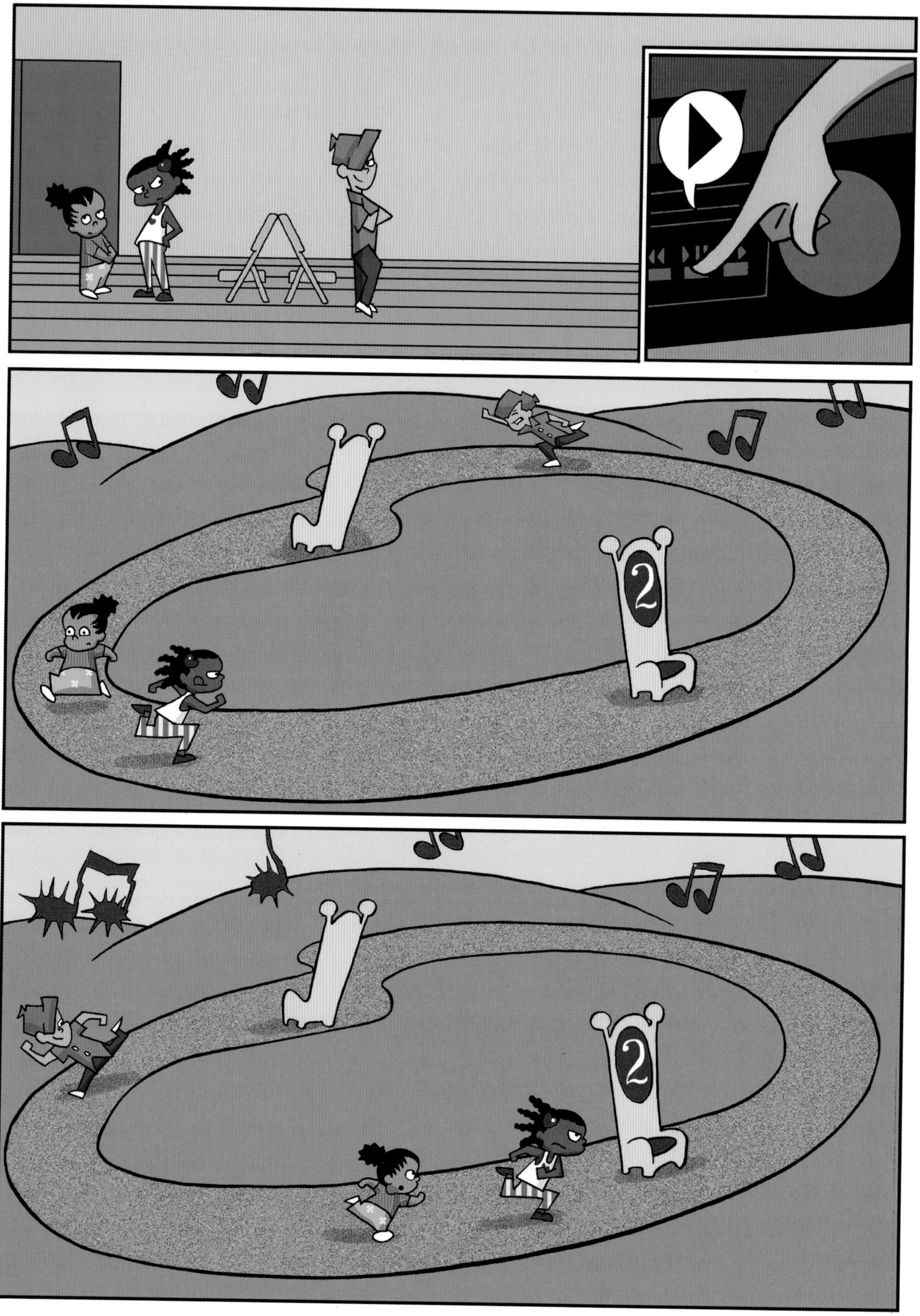
2
2
2

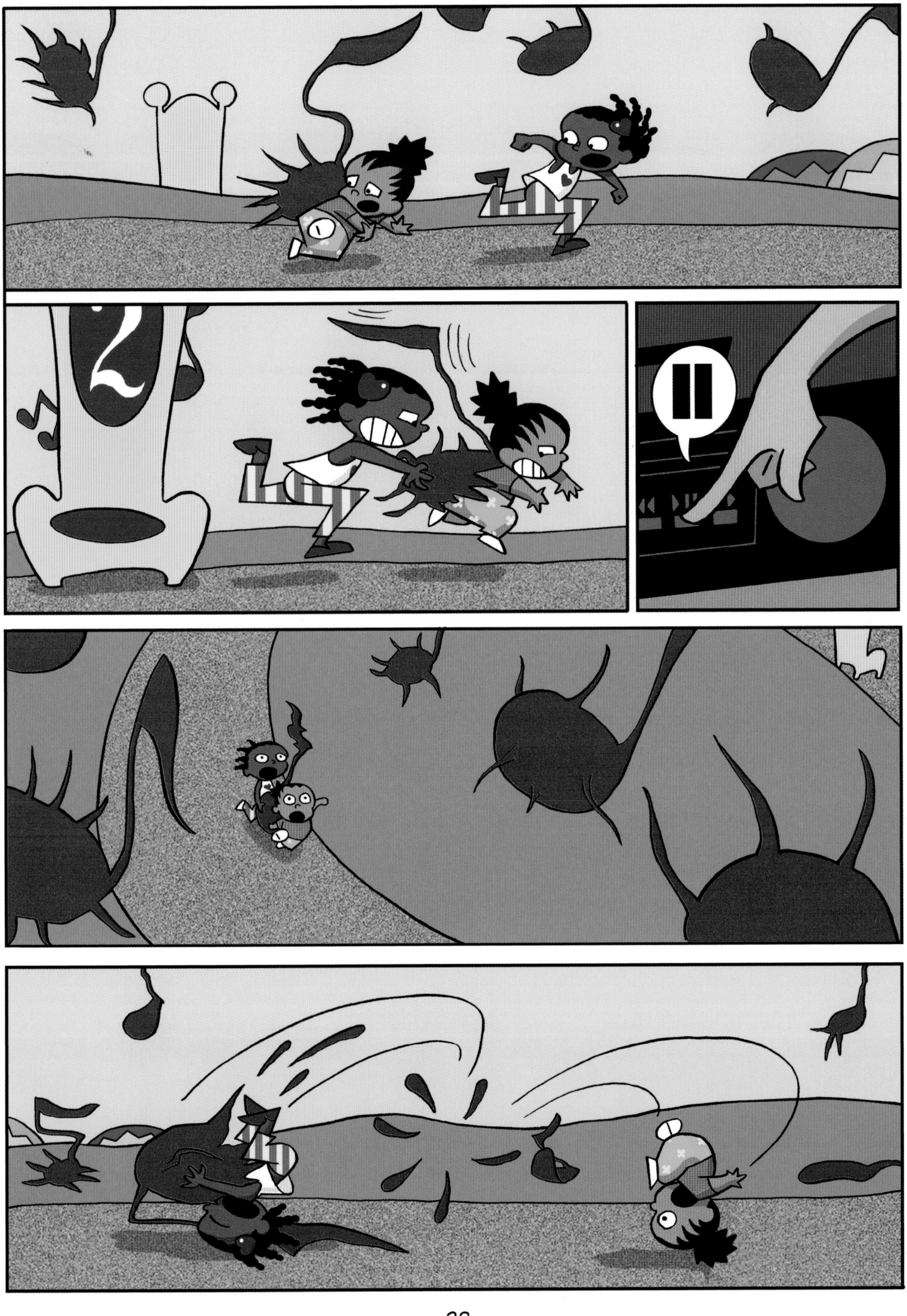

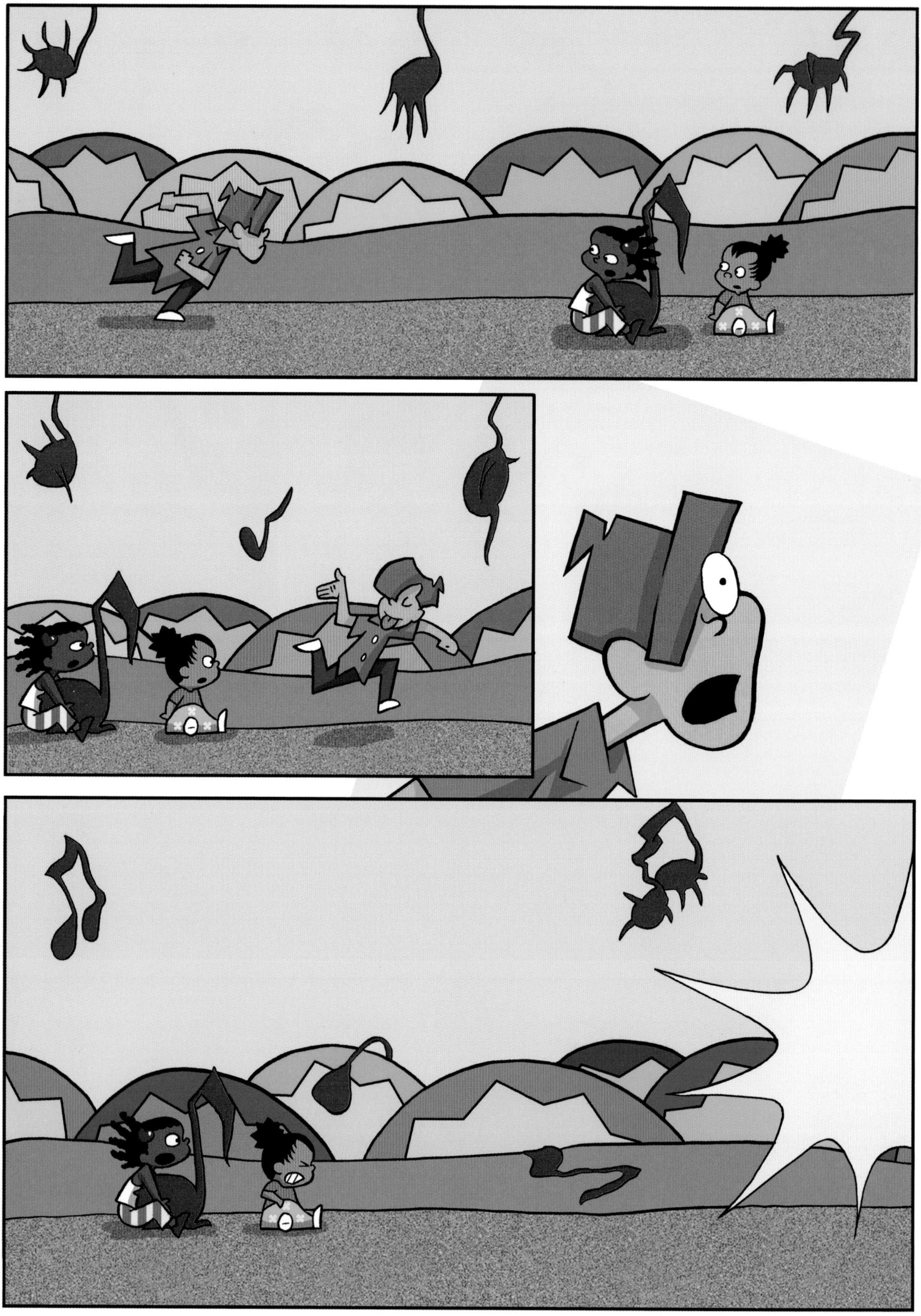

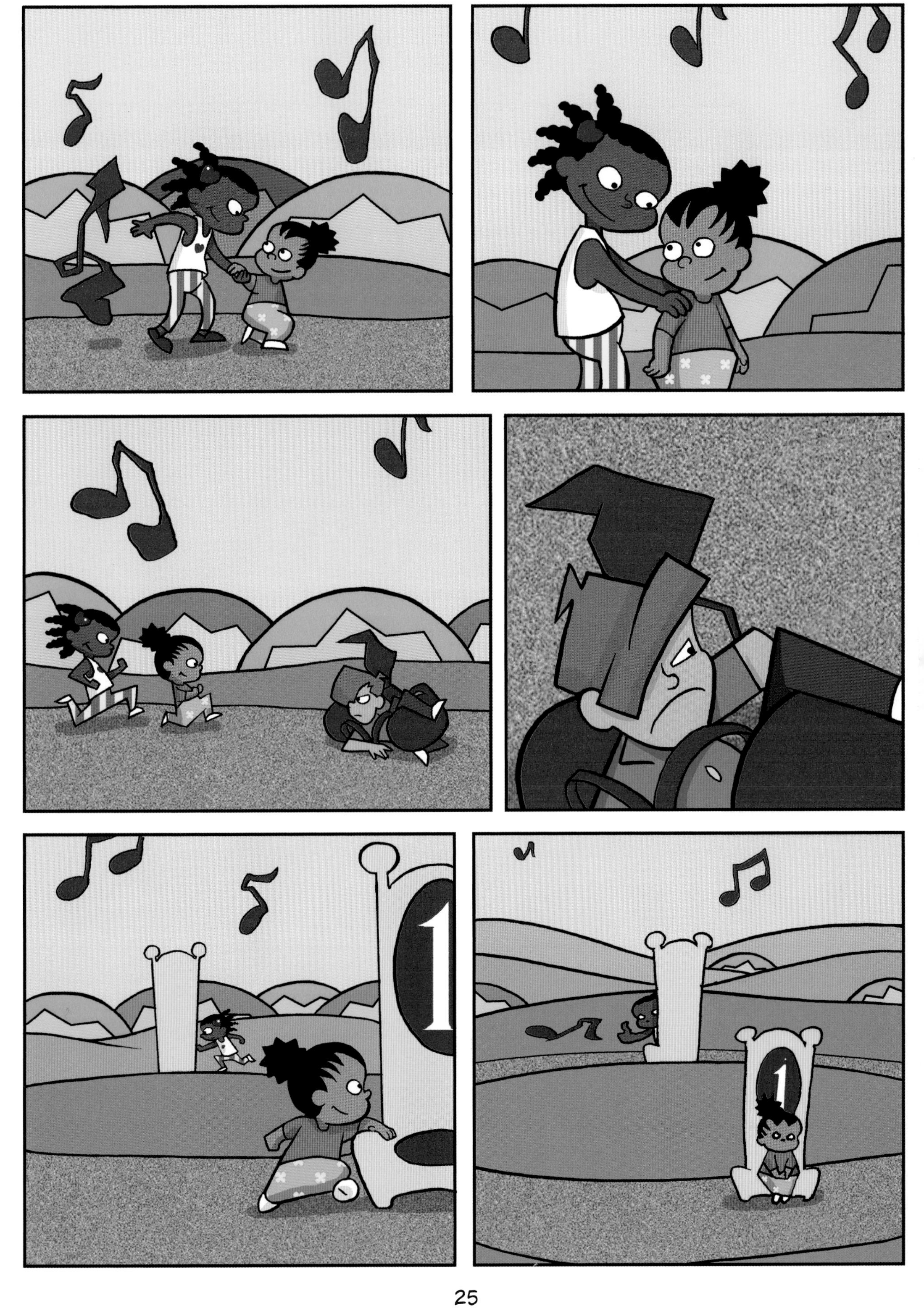
1
1

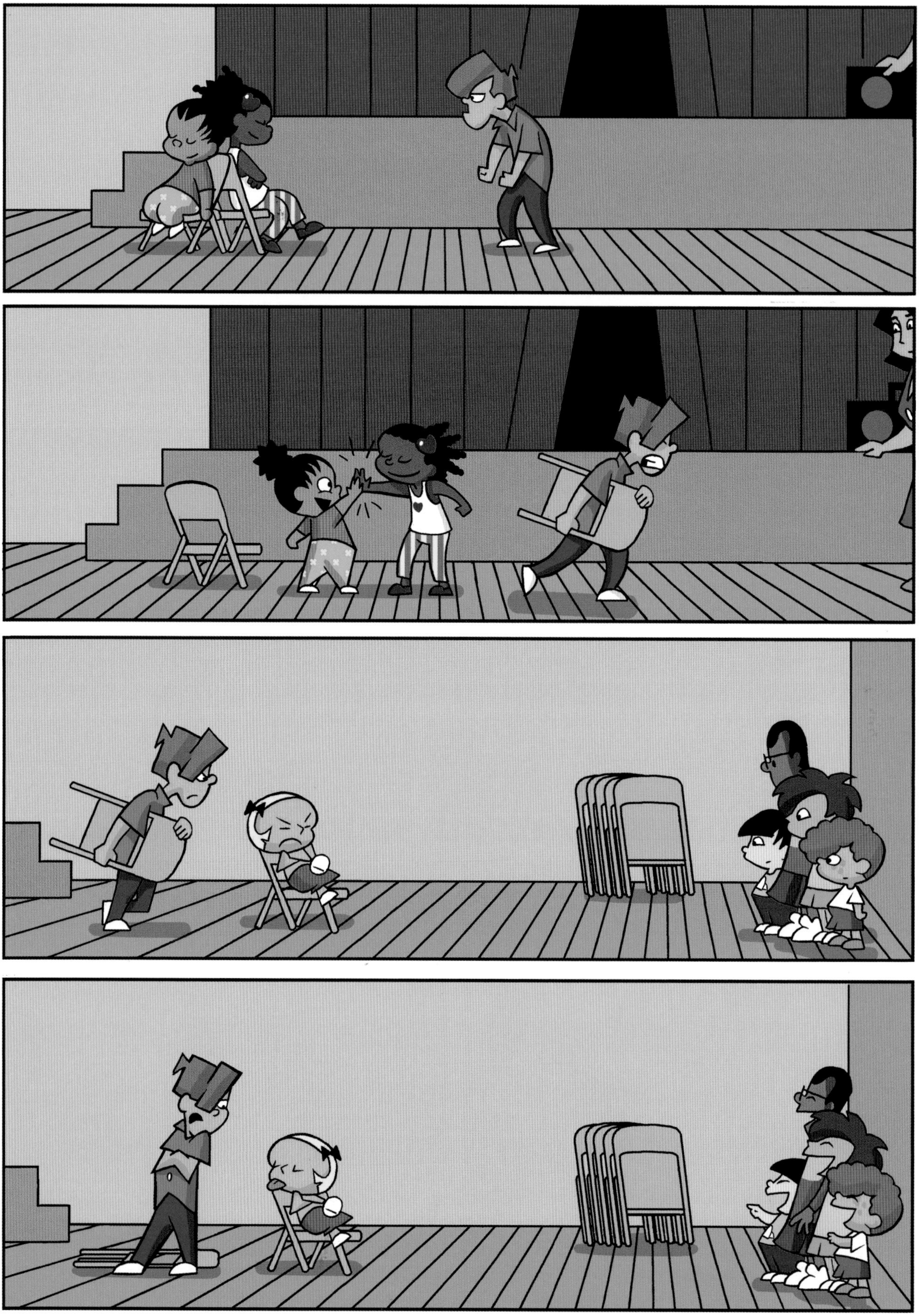

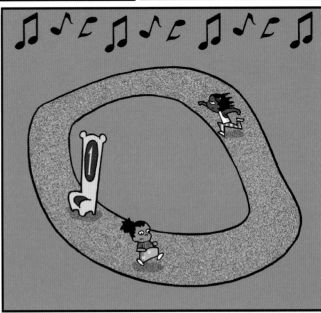

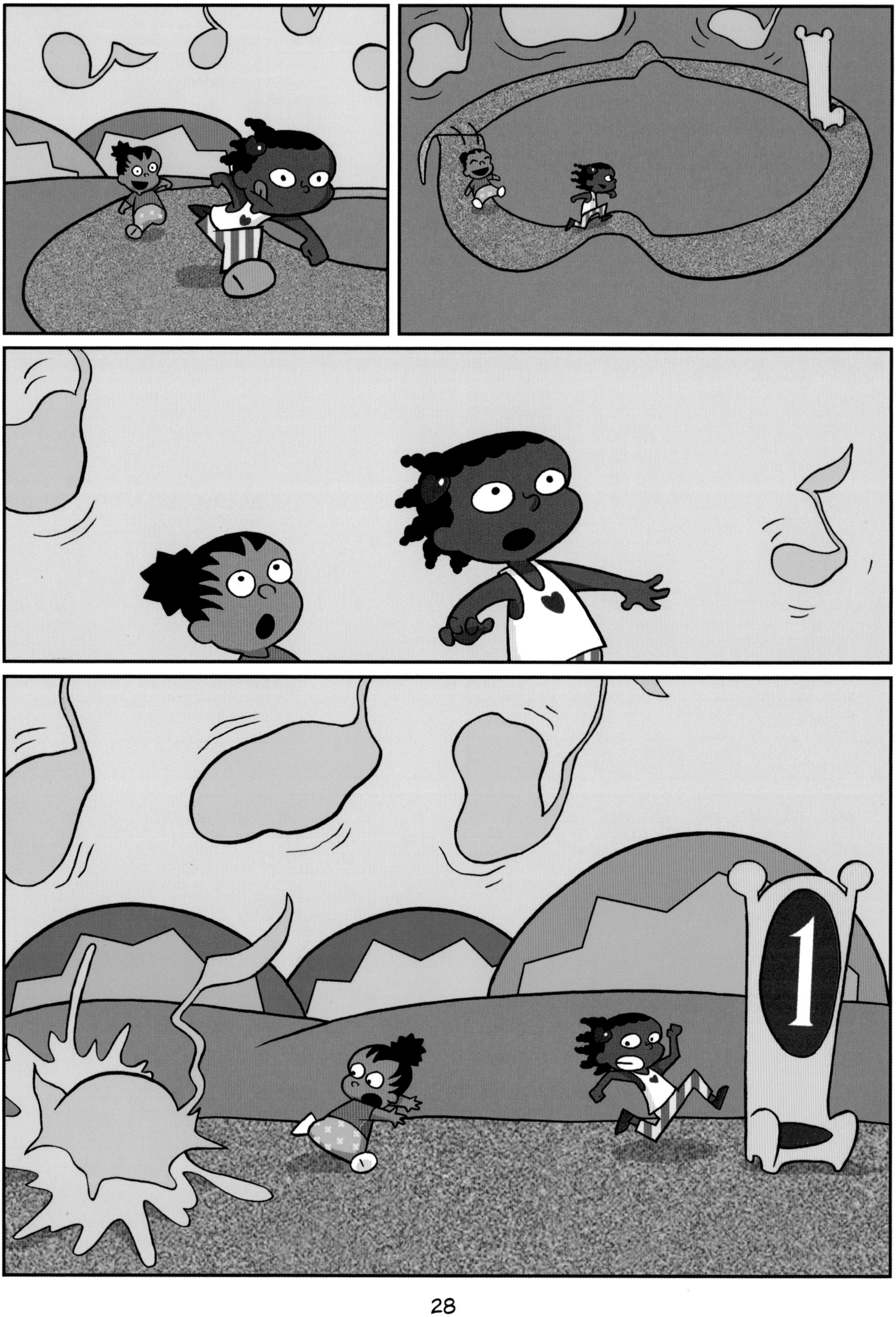
1

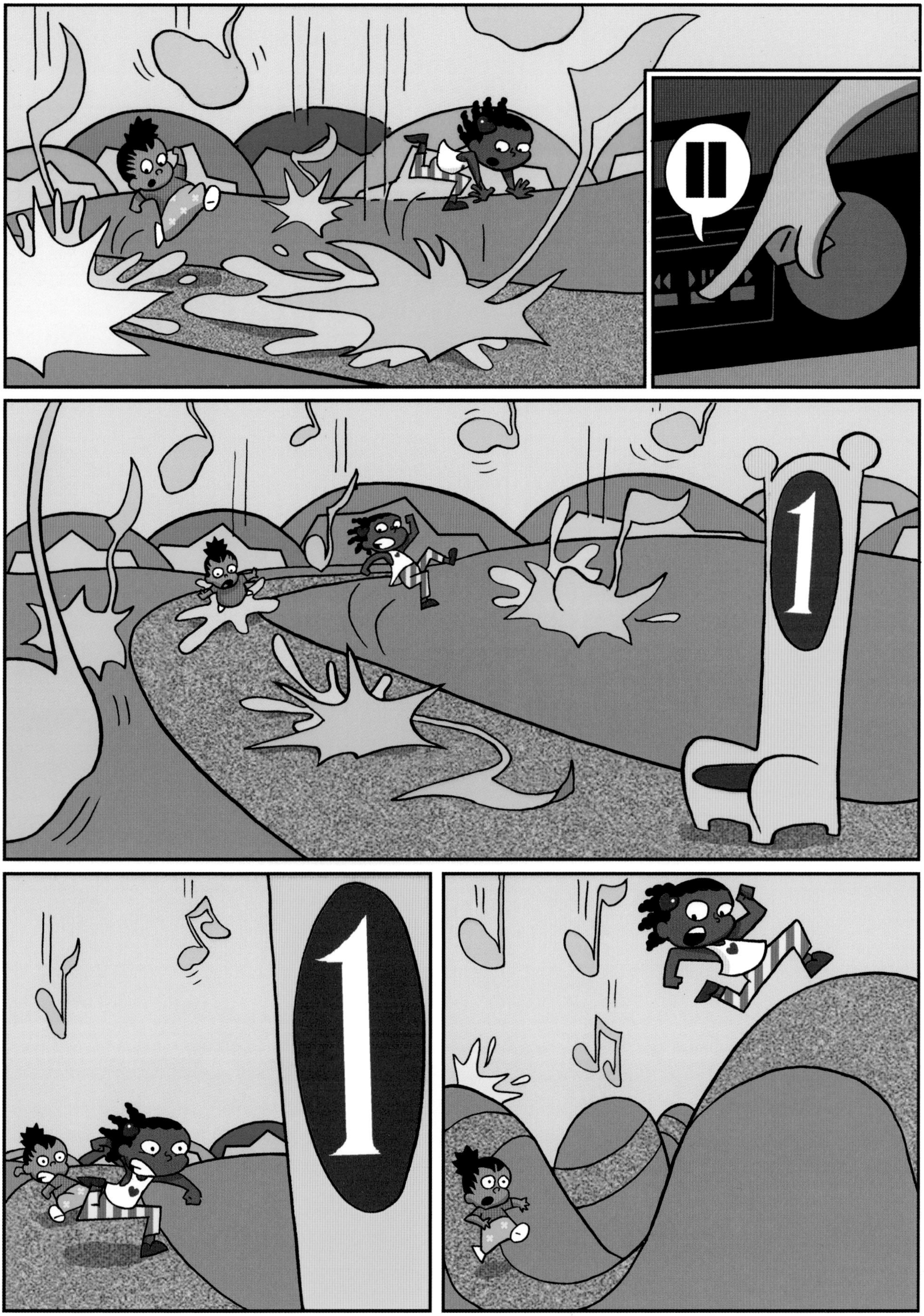
1

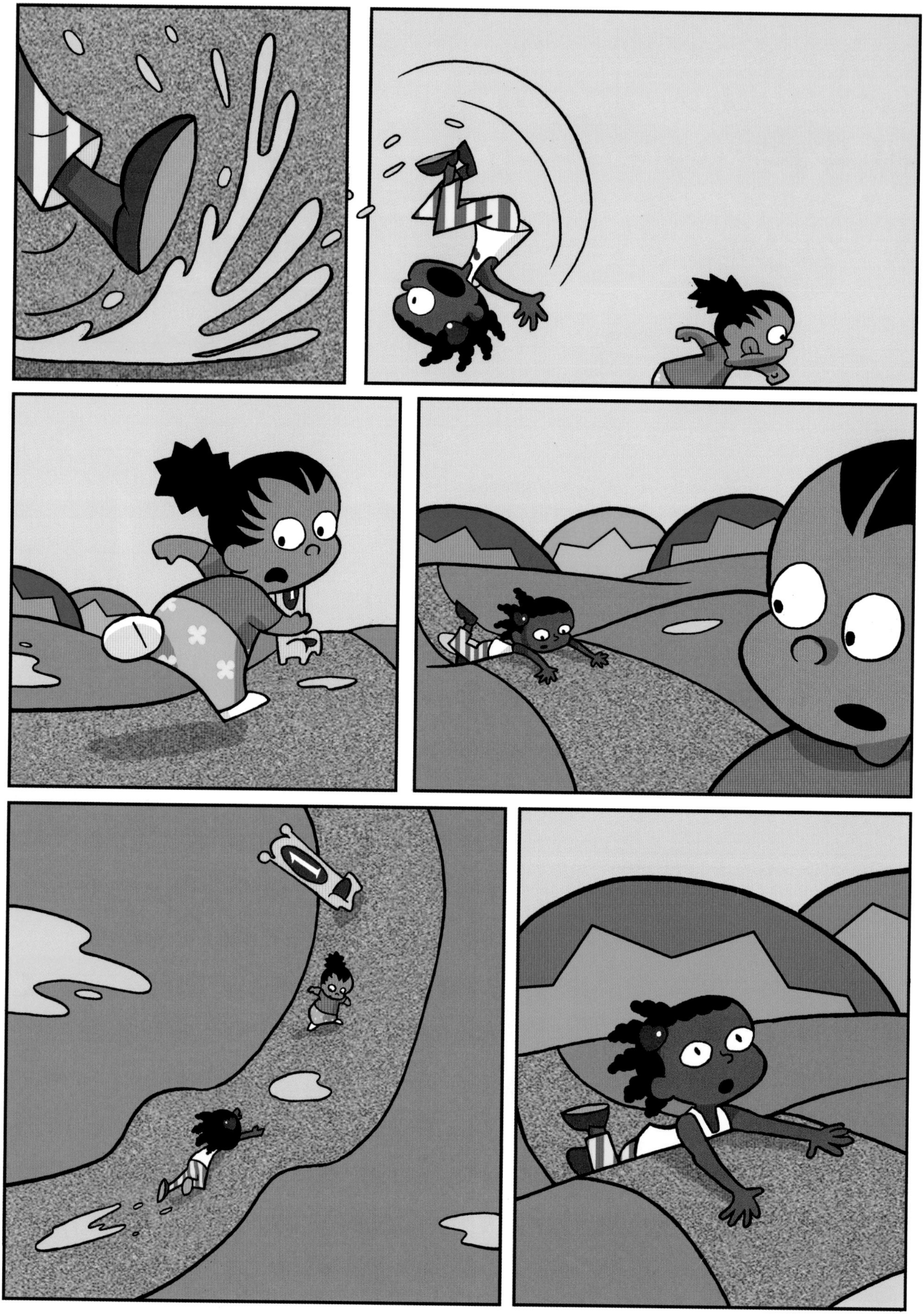

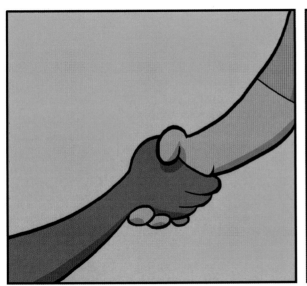

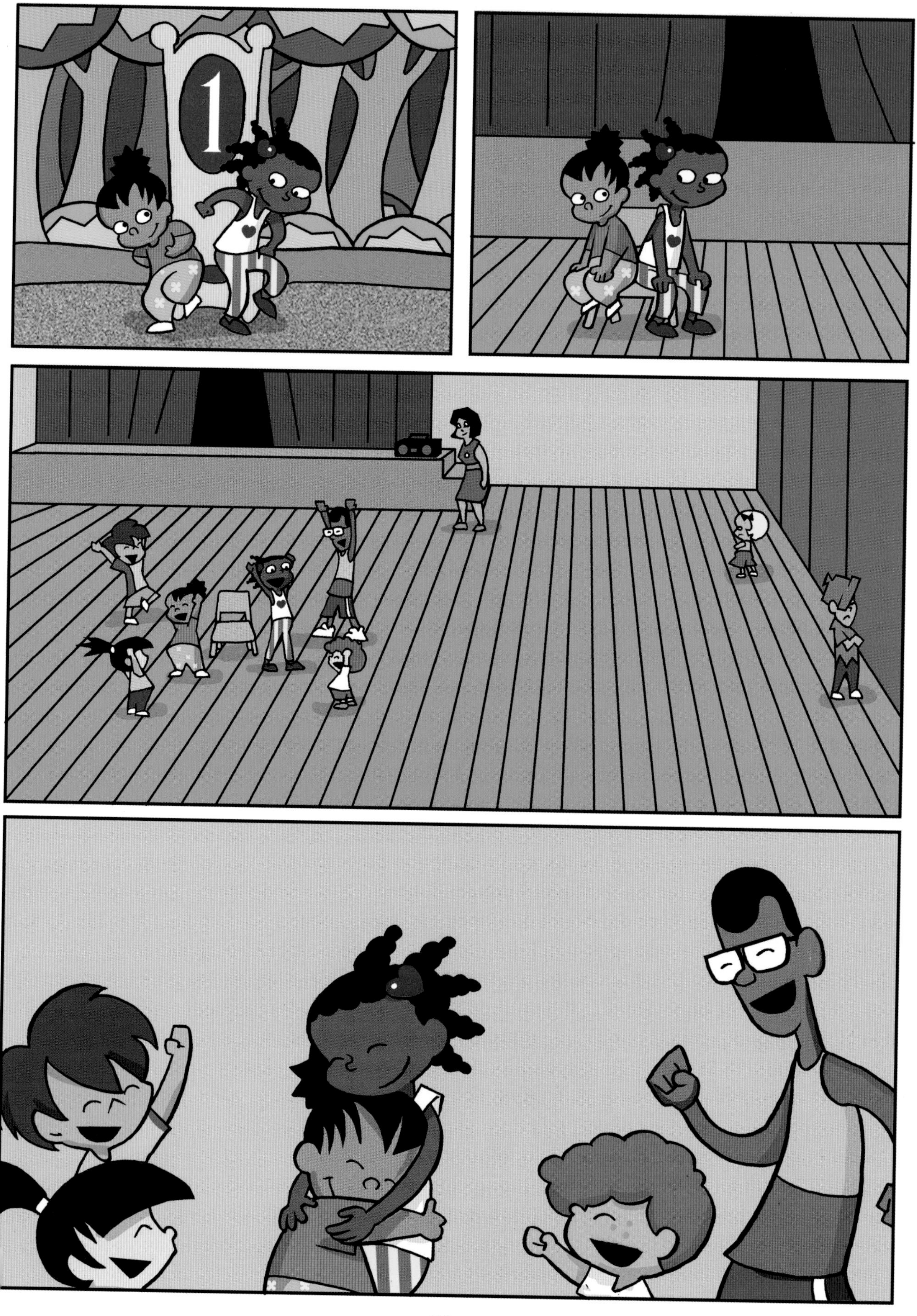

THE END

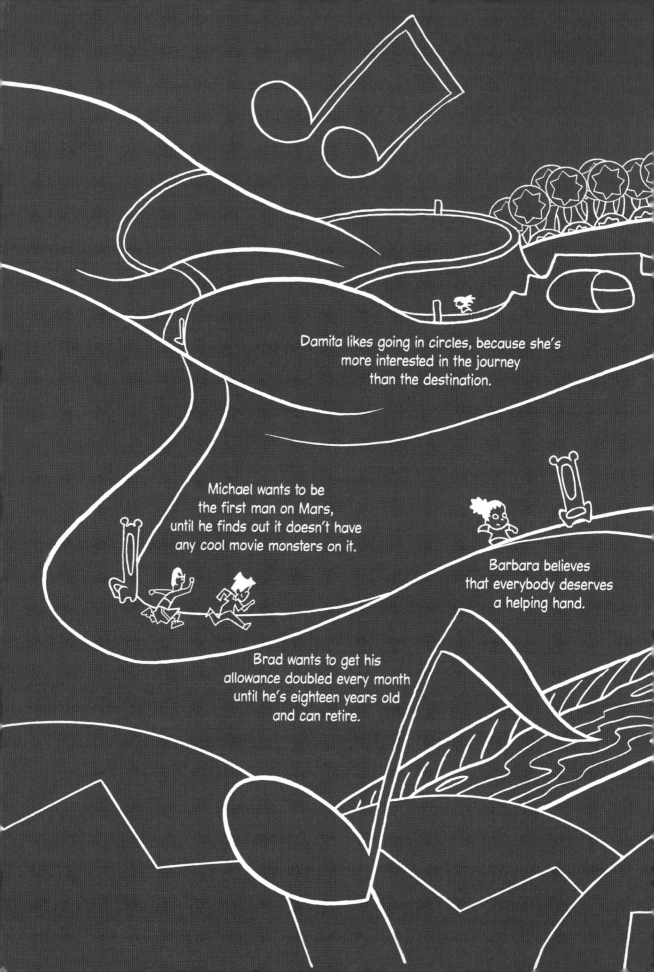

Damita likes going in circles, because she's more interested in the journey than the destination.

Michael wants to be the first man on Mars, until he finds out it doesn't have any cool movie monsters on it.

Barbara believes that everybody deserves a helping hand.

Brad wants to get his allowance doubled every month until he's eighteen years old and can retire.

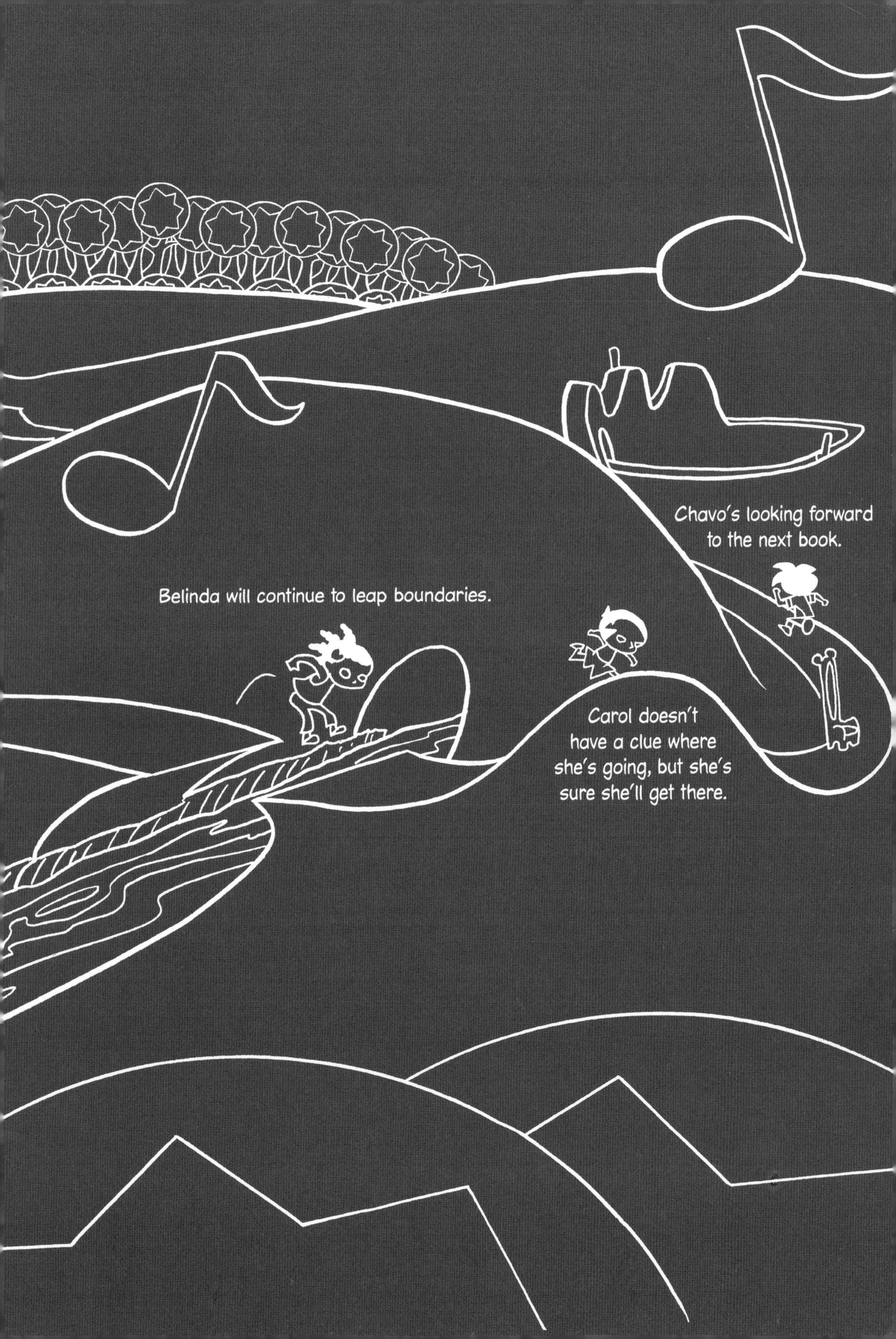
Chavo's looking forward to the next book.
Belinda will continue to leap boundaries.
Carol doesn't have a clue where she's going, but she's sure she'll get there.